Hey Crazy Riddle!

To Jennifer

Happy Reading

Love

Trish Cooke

TC.

With thanks to my Mum and Dad,
Agnes and Abiah Hewlett Cooke.
Also V. Spalding who helped through her grandson,
my nephew Jason.

Hey Crazy Riddle! copyright © Frances Lincoln Limited 2006
Text copyright © Trish Cooke 2006
Illustrations copyright © Hannah Shaw 2006

First published in Great Britain and the USA in 2006 by
Frances Lincoln Children's Books, 4 Torriano Mews,
Torriano Avenue, London NW5 2RZ

www.franceslincoln.com

Distributed in the USA by Publishers Group West

British Library Cataloguing in Publication Data
available on request

ISBN 10: 1-84507-378-9
ISBN 13: 978-84507-378-7

Printed in the United Kingdom

1 3 5 7 9 8 6 4 2

Hey Crazy Riddle!

Trish Cooke

Illustrated by Hannah Shaw

F

FRANCES LINCOLN
CHILDREN'S BOOKS

Note from the author

Though I was born in Yorkshire, England,
my mother and father are from Dominica
in the West Indies. When I retell these stories
I can hear my father's mischievous voice
teasing as he used to when he told me stories,
always joking around. Some of the stories
don't rhyme and sometimes the rhythms
are not regular but that is part of the
colourful way that stories are told in the
Caribbean, so don't worry if you stumble.
Have fun and enjoy!

Contents

Why Agouti Has No Tail

*Do you know why
Agouti has no tail?
Well...*

Bull was having a party, a party on a boat.
He sent out special invitations to the animals
    who could go.

"Don't matter what colour you are,
could be pink, or blue or brown.
Only thing you need to be
is an animal with a horn."

Well, Dog had no horn you see,
so he thought that was unfair.
He needed to find a horn for the party.
"There must be one somewhere!"

Now Goat was sick at home in bed.
Dog thought that he would visit.

"If Goat is sick, then he won't need his horn.
He can do without it!"

Dog brought Goat chocolates and flowers,
and he never mentioned the party once.
They talked and talked for hours and hours,
until Goat fell asleep.

Then Dog took Goat's horn
    and left.

Now Agouti had been watching from outside,
and when he saw Dog with Goat's horn
Agouti walked by Dog's side.

"What's going on?" said Agouti.
"That horn does not belong to you!"
"It does tonight!" said Dog.
    "So what is it to you?"

Agouti followed Dog down the track.
"That horn belongs to Goat!"
For Dog there was no turning back,
and he got on to the boat.

But when Agouti tried to get on board
    the guards said,
"Get off! You have no horn!"
So he watched all the party animals
as they danced and danced 'til dawn.

Now, jealous Agouti had an idea.
He jumped up and down and he called,
"Check out your horns, Mr Bull, my friend!
You have an impostor on board!"

"Impostor?" said Bull.
"Impostor on here?
Round up my guests!
Impostor? Where?
Where?"

Dog was frightened
but did not show it.
He lined up with the others,
his horn firmly fixed.

"Is this your horn?"
each animal was asked,
and each animal
answered, "YES!"
Then the guard
gave a tug just
to make sure
that the animal who spoke
was not a liar!

But when the guard got
to the end of the line
Dog was trembling.
"Sir, this horn is not mine!"
As the guard tried to catch him,
Dog ran off,
saw Agouti and grabbed him
and he bit his tail off!

*... And that
is why Agouti
has no tail.*

Why Wasp Can't Make Honey

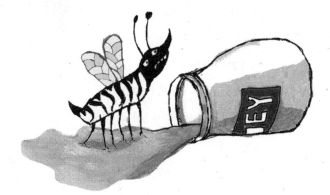

*Do you know why
Wasp can't make honey?
Well...*

Oh, Bee was a busy bee,
always busy making honey,
making honey for everybody.
Yes, Bee was a busy bee.

Yes, Bee was a busy bee
but still had time
    for everybody.
Said "Good morning"
    to the whole community,
as he went about
    his daily duty.

But Wasp was a rush-rush wasp,
doing nothing yet always in a rush.
"Can't stop, I'm... *mmmmmmmmm,*"
    he would say,
and then he would be on his way.

Yes, Wasp was a rush-rush wasp,
always rushing, always in a hurry.
Face always scrunched up like he's
    full of worry.
Yes, Wasp was always in a hurry!

Every day was the same old thing.
"Can't stop! I'm... *mmmmmmmmm,*"
    went the hum of Wasp's wing.
While Bee visited flowers and collected
    nectar for his honey,
Wasp whizzed around.
Yes, always in a hurry.

When Bee finished, he took time off
   for resting.
Wasp would still be humming by,
   rushing doing nothing.

But one day Wasp grew tired
   of whizzing here
   and there,
   and he called to Bee,
   "Friend, I need
   a chair!"
   And Bee found Wasp
   the sweetest flower
   for him to have
   a snooze.
   Then Bee went about
   his business,
   while Wasp had a doze.
   Wasp watched Bee though he
   was snoring
   zzzzzzzzzzz,
   one eye open, then he begged,
   "That look good what you are making.
   Can I try a bit?" he said.

17

So
Bee gave Wasp some of his honey.
"*Mmmmmm,*" said Wasp.
"*Yummmmmmeeeee,*
    yummmmmmeeeee."
"If you care to wait a moment,
I'll give you the recipe,"
said Bee.

Wasp quickly ate off all Bee's honey but
he didn't wait around.
In the distance Bee could hear that
old familiar sound.
"Can't stop, I'm... *mmmmmmmmm
mmmmmmmmm mmmmmmmmm!*"

*... And that is why
Wasp can't make honey –
too much in a hurry!*

Why Dog Barks

Do you know
why Dog barks?
Well ...

Two brothers, Danny and Ben,
were building a house –
a kind of a den.
They worked very hard to make it just right.
Worked through the day and through
    the night.
And then when they had just the roof
    to put on,
they stopped for a rest.

Along
came a man,
a man and his dog,
and he said,
"My friends,
when will the house be finished?"
And they said,
"Tomorrow, for sure."

"Tomorrow for sure?"
laughed the man,
and the house came
tumbling down.

Just collapsed,
right there to the ground.

The brothers were shocked.
"How could this be?"
Yet they started to build it again.

Two brothers, Danny and Ben,
were building a house –
a kind of a den.
They worked very hard
    to make it just right.
Worked through the day
    and through the night.

And then when they had
        just the roof to put on,
they stopped for a rest.

Then along came a man,
    a man and his dog,
and he asked them again,
"When will the house be finished,
        my friends?"
And they said,
"Tomorrow, for sure."

"Tomorrow for sure?" laughed the man
    once again,
and the house came tumbling down.
Just collapsed,
right there to the ground.

The brothers were shocked.
"How could this be?"
Yet they started to build
    it again.

As the man walked away
he spoke to his dog.
"What a fool
    is a man
who thinks
    he knows all.

For nobody knows for sure
what tomorrow may bring.
One can only hope
for the best of everything."

But the dog felt sorry for Danny and Ben.
So he waited for the man
to go to sleep.
Then he crept
to where the brothers were building
and said,
"Next time my master asks you
when your house will be finished,
don't say tomorrow for sure,
for nobody knows for sure what tomorrow
    may bring.
Tell him you will finish when the time
    is right."

The brothers thanked the dog and went
    to sleep.
Two brothers, Danny and Ben,
were building a house –
a kind of a den.

They worked very hard to make it just right.
Worked through the day and through
    the night.
And then when they had just the roof to
    put on,
they stopped for a rest.

Then along came a man,
a man and his dog,
and he asked them again,
"When will the house be finished,
    my friends?"
And remembering what the dog had
    told them, they said,
"The house will be finished when the time
    is right."
"You talk too much, Dog," said the man.
"But for giving them the answer you will
    never talk again."
"Woof!" said the dog, because that's all
    he could say,
and as the man and the dog turned to
    walk away,
the brothers began to put on the roof,
and before long the house was finished.

*... And that is why
Dog barks.*

Why Cockerel Crows

*Do you know
why Cockerel crows?
Well...*

Every morning bright and early
    as the day breaks,
Ko ki o ko! Ko ki o ko!
Hear his call, make no mistake, it's him,
Ko ki o ko! Ko ki o ko!
He struts his walk,
Ko ki o ko! Ko ki o ko!
He clucks his cluck,
Ko ki o ko! Ko ki o ko!
Oh, what a day, what a glorious day,
Ko ki o ko! Ko ki o ko!
Ko ki o ko! Ko ki o ko!
But
it wasn't always so...

In days of old,
    any time you saw Cockerel,
        he was cross.
    Nothing could please Cockerel.
    Yes, Cockerel was miserable.

The sun would shine,
he would say,
"Cha! Man, the sun
    making me hot.
    Give me some rain!"

Rain would fall,
he would say,
"Cha! See how the rain
wetting me. Give me
        some wind!"

The wind would blow,
he would say,
"Cha! Feel that draught. Give me some sun!"
And no matter what the weather
you just could not please Cockerel.

"Cha! Man, the sun making me hot. Give me
    some rain!"
"Cha! See how the rain wetting me. Give me
    some wind!"
"Cha! Feel that draught. Give me some sun!"

And after a while,
Weather stopped bothering with Cockerel
and Weather started to please herself.

She made the sun shine when she wanted to.
She sprinkled rain whenever she liked,
and the wind blew when the fancy took her.

And the more Cockerel
complained
about the sun making
him hot,
the rain wetting him,
and the draughty wind,
the more Weather did as she pleased.
Until...
she made Cockerel so hot, so wet
and so miserable
that he called out to her,
"Mistress Weather, I'm sorry.
Please can we go back to the way things
were before?
I promise I won't complain again ever!"

"What shall you do instead?" said Weather.
"I'll praise you every day," said Cockerel.

And that's exactly what he does to this day.

Every morning bright and early as the
    day breaks,
Ko ki o ko! Ko ki o ko!
Hear his call, make no mistake, it's him,
Ko ki o ko! Ko ki o ko!
He struts his walk,
Ko ki o ko! Ko ki o ko!
He clucks his cluck,
Ko ki o ko! Ko ki o ko!
Oh, what a day, what a glorious day,
Ko ki o ko! Ko ki o ko!
Ko ki o ko! Ko ki o ko!

*... And that is
why Cockerel crows.*

How Dog Lost His Bone

*Do you know
how Dog lost his bone?
Well ...*

Woof Dog has a bone,
bone all right,
he plays with the bone,
all day, all night.
Licking bone,
and chewing bone.
Woof Dog and
his bone are cool!

Woof Dog sees a river,
looking good.
Woof Dog takes his bone,
and has a look.

Water rippling,
water bright,
Woof Dog sees another dog in the water.
Oh, oh,
Woof Dog wants to have a fight!

Woof Dog wants to dive in the river
cos the other dog has a bone that's bigger.

Woof Dog leaps into the water.
What a bouncer!
What a splash!
The other dog has gone
from the water!
Oh, oh, Woof Dog
starts to laugh!

There was no other dog
in the river.
The face he'd seen had been his own.
The water made him shake and shiver,
and now he'd lost his juicy bone!

What a fool,
not so cool.
But Woof Dog still rules!
OK!

*... And that is how Dog
lost his bone.*

How Goat Got More

*Do you know
how Goat got more?
Well ...*

Cabwit Goat had a very big appetite.
No matter what he ate
    he always wanted more.
His belly would rumble and roar
and he would say,
"I want more, I want more!"
But there was never any more
    than what he had.
And that was his problem.

"If only I could hatch a plan
to fill my belly," he would say.
And that's all he thought about
    night and day.

As he ate his breakfast
    he grumbled,
"I want more, I want more!"
When he ate his dinner
    he cried,
"I want more, I want more!"

And when he ate
his supper
he moaned,
"I want more,
  I want more!"

No sah, Cabwit
   Goat was
   never satisfied
   with what he had.
   He couldn't even
see what he had.
If anybody asked him what he had for
   breakfast,
he didn't even know because
his mind was too fixed on what he didn't have.
"I want more, I want more!" he would say.
Every day the same thing.

Until one day Cwapo Frog was so tired
   of his foolishness,
he asked Cabwit Goat,
"More of what?"

"I don't know," said Cabwit Goat.
"Just more than what I'm getting."

"I don't have much," said Cwapo Frog,
"but I'm so tired of you going on about
what you don't have.
Why don't you come and have some dinner
with me and my family on Sunday?
My wife's a good cook.
If she cannot satisfy you, no one can."

Cabwit Goat could not believe his luck.
"Thank you, Cwapo Frog," he said.
"I'll be there Sunday."
And just as he was leaving, Cabwit Goat
    had an idea.
"Cwapo Frog," Cabwit Goat said,
"is it all right for me to bring a friend?"
"Which friend?" said Cwapo Frog,
because he had never seen Cabwit Goat
    with any friends.
"You don't have any."
"Oh, there is one," said Cabwit Goat,
"He doesn't come out often,
but I was expecting him for dinner on Sunday.
And since I'm going to be at your house
I may as well bring him with me."

"Oh," said Cwapo Frog.
    "Well, I don't know.
See I have such a big family,
six growing boys and
    three young girls,
then there's my mother,
the wife's mother and father

and the wife has to eat too.
I really don't know if there'll be enough
    for one more."
"I've heard your wife is the best cook
    in these parts,"
said Cabwit Goat. "Everybody knows it.
In fact every time I see my friend Skolar,
that is all we ever talk about.
He would be overjoyed
to come and have a meal at your house."

Cwapo Frog puffed up with pride.
So pleased was he that everyone thought
    so highly of his wife's cooking.

                Next thing he knew,
                    he was telling Cabwit Goat
                how his friend Skolar would
                    be more than welcome
                to join them for dinner.
                "OK," he said, "come
                    with your friend.
                    See you Sunday."
                And that was that.

Cabwit Goat danced all the way home.
When he ate his dinner that day he laughed,
  ha ha ha.
When he ate his supper he sang,
  zubby zubby zum.
Next day, the same thing,
ha ha ha,
zubby zubby zum.

And the next,
and the next,
until Sunday finally arrived.

Cabwit Goat dressed in a fine suit
and he skipped all the way
    to Cwapo Frog's home.
He knocked on the door, *toke toke toke.*
"Let me in," he said. "Let me in.
I can smell your wife lovely dinner cooking!"
And Cwapo Frog opened the door for him.

"Hello, Cabwit Goat. Welcome to my home,"
said Cwapo Frog looking behind Cabwit Goat.
"But where is your friend?
My wife cooked an extra portion especially
     for him.
Don't say he's not coming."
"Oh, he's coming," said Cabwit Goat.
"He just had a bit of business to take care of.
He told me to say sorry to your lovely wife.
He won't be long now," Cabwit Goat said.
"Skolar soon come."

Then Cabwit Goat made himself at home,
     playing with the children.

All the time his eyes on
the big pot of food
on the stove
and his nose
in the air,
smelling the
lovely meal
cooking.

"*Mmmmmm*, smell good," he said, licking
his lips.
"What time we eating?"
"As soon as your friend arrives,"
said Madam Cwapo Frog.
Cabwit Goat said, "We may as well sit down
at the table
because he'll be here any minute.
I know my mate Skolar soon come."

The Cwapo children were hungry
and so Cwapo Frog agreed.
"Go to the table, children," he said,
"and when our final guest arrives, we'll eat."

So everyone sat at the table and waited.

Cabwit Goat checked the time
and made like he was looking for his friend
through the window.
Every minute he was saying,
"But where is he nah?"
But there was no sign of Skolar.

"The dinner smells good," said Cabwit Goat.
"When are you going to dish it out?"
"As soon as your friend arrives,"
said Madam Cwapo Frog.

"You could dish out now.
Just put his dish next to mine
and when he come we'll be all ready to eat.
Won't be long now. Skolar soon come."
"Well," said Cwapo Frog. "I suppose
        we could do."
So Madam Cwapo Frog put out the dishes
and an extra one beside Cabwit Goat,
        for his friend Skolar.
When all the food was in the dishes,
Cabwit Goat checked the time again.

"The food's going to get cold,"
        said Cabwit Goat.
"It would be a shame
        not to eat this
        food hot
after Madam Cwapo
        Frog has spent
        so much time
        preparing
            it."

"We'll give him a few more minutes,"
        said Madam Cwapo Frog.
"That's OK," said Cabwit Goat, "because
        Skolar soon come."

But after waiting a few more minutes
there was still no sign of Cabwit Goat's friend,
        Skolar.

"Maybe," said Cabwit Goat,
" we should start eating and when Skolar come
        he can join us."

"I'll put his on the stove to keep warm,"
        said Madam Cwapo Frog.
But before she could take Skolar's dish,
Cabwit Goat grabbed it. "No, no. It's all right
        where it is.
Skolar prefers it
        cool," he
said.

Then the whole family
and Cabwit Goat
tucked into the fine meal Madam Cwapo Frog
    had cooked for them
but there was still no sign of Cabwit Goat's
    friend, Skolar.
Time and time again, Cabwit Goat looked at
    his watch
and made like he was looking to see where
    his friend had got to,
and each time he checked the dish of food
    next to him.

"Maybe he not coming again?"
    said Madam Cwapo Frog.
"It is getting late," said Cwapo Frog.
"It's almost time to get the children to bed,"
    said Madam Cwapo Frog.
"No, he mustn't be coming again,"
    said Cwapo Frog.

"Maybe you're right," said Cabwit Goat.
"And it would be such a shame
to let this lovely food go to waste," he said,
emptying Skolar's food into his mouth.

"Some people," said Cabwit Goat,
    "are just so rude!"

*... And that is how
Goat got more.*

Hey Crazy Riddle!

Hey, Kitty Twiddle,
the cat played the fiddle.
She played from morning
and played 'til noon.
Fiddlee-dee and fiddlee-day.
All the time she wanted to play.
Everybody say,
"What do that cat!
Cat, you making too much noise!
Cat, go away. Go away. Go away!"

The cat say,
   "*Me owwwww owwww owwww.*"
And the string on the fiddle say
   PING!

               Every string make a ping
               and a ping
               and a ping.

      So the cat say, "I may as well sing!"
      Well, what a thing, that cat sing.
      She meowww 'til me ears
         dem a-ring!

Hey, Daisy Fuddle,
the cat and the fiddle,
the cow *tried* to jump over the moon.

But the moon was too low
and the cow didn't know.
Nearly knocked
    herself senseless
and nobody know
that the cow bang her
    head on the moon.
No, no,
nobody know,
but everybody will know soon.

Hey, Puppy Giggle,
the cat and the fiddle,
the cow *almost* jumped over the moon.
The little dog laughed
but that dog was so daft.
Ask him why he laugh, he don't know.
He just skin back his teeth and hold up
    his belly,
and laugh, *tee hee*,
    tee hee.
What a fool-fool dog
was he!

Hey, Tasty Nibble,

the cat and the fiddle,

the cow *nearly* jumped over the moon.

And that little fool-fool dog just giggle

while the dish, well –

what a muddle!

You see,

the fork was good friends with the dish.

The knife say him and the dish were

    good buddies.

All of them did get on well

    with the dish,

but the dish say,

"I so sorry.

You see I have a date with the custard curdler,

the lip-smacking soup slurper,
the peaches-and-cream dipper,
the sugar-in-tea
    (sweet little old thing) stirrer!
I have a date with the spoon, so there!
I have a date with the spoon!"

Hey, Crazy Riddle,
the cat play the fiddle,
the cow
try so hard, I tell you,
she try so hard to clear that moon but
    it wasn't to be
and the dog laugh *tee hee*,
like somebody give him joke.
Yes, somebody really give that dog joke!
And you know,
although it was a big surprise to everyone,
it *was* the dish
yes, the dish, that talked the spoon into
running away with her.
Yes, the spoon
ran away with the dish!

... And that's no lie!

Funny Langwig